For Kathleen —
keep on with your
strong writing —
Best wishes —
Shirley Cochrane
June '92

EVERYTHING THAT'S ALL

EVERYTHING THAT'S ALL

1930-1942

by Shirley Graves Cochrane

Printed in the United States of America.

Acknowledgments

Cover illustration by Wm. D. Cochrane Copyright © 1991.

Book design and artwork by Michael Brown.

The title story, "Everything That's All," was a PEN/Syndicated Fiction winner and appeared in the Chapel Hill, NC, *Village Advocate* and the St. Petersburg, FL, *Times*.
The character Charlie Mock was introduced in a story that appeared in the *Ladies' Home Journal*, and he and other characters and episodes were first presented there, in different form.
Permission to quote the lyrics of M-O-T-H-E-R, by Howard Johnson, has been granted by CCP/Belwin, Inc.
The photographs of the Carolina Trailways busses and of the Tommy Dorsey dance, courtesy of the Photographic Division, Louis Round Wilson Library, University of North Carolina.
The photograph of the *Memphis Belle* reproduced from the Collections of the Library of Congress.
The photograph of the 1940 Hudson super-six convertible, courtesy of Joseph H. Knox.

Library of Congress Cataloging-in-Publication Data

Cochrane, Shirley, 1925-
    Everything that's all (1930-1942)/Shirley Graves Cochrane.

    ISBN: 0-930095-07-3 : $16.50
    I. Title.
    PS3553.027E94   1991
    813' .54—dc20   91-10617
                                           CIP

For My Family --
Bill, Dan, Tom, and Suzanne

CONTENTS

Chapter 1

1930

EVERYTHING THAT'S ALL

Today I'm going downtown to buy me
a baby. I've got the money from my Red
Devil lye bank. Buffalo nickels and mer-
cury dimes, all the pennies but the Indian
heads. It's the second time I've saved it up.
The first time I gave the money to Mama
when she had to go to court for backing into
the car of the bootlegger's daughter, who

was waving at friends and not looking where she was going. And when the bootlegger came over to our house to talk to Mama, I tried to bite him on the leg. So to make up to Mama for all the expense and heartbreak she went through then, I gave her my money. But I've saved it back up and now I can get the baby.

This is the first time I've walked to town by myself. No one knows I'm gone. Charlie Mae was supposed to be watching me, but she got so interested in the cat book she let me slip away. I've cut through the lilac jungle and have two blocks of houses to go. After the houses comes the Spinning Wheel Shop — Candy, Cakes and Pastries, Afternoon Tea. Sometimes Granny stands at the front door telling her customers goodbye. But today she's over in Durham buying milk chocolate slabs and glassine candy cups. Allie is at the counter but not looking out. Allie is Charlie Mae's older sister. Flora is their mother and also our

2

housekeeper who helps raise me while Granny runs the Spinning Wheel Shop and Mama runs her office. My mama is a widow lady.

So now I'm in the block where Plyler's Five and Dime is. A sign reads *Everything That's All*. I go in and Mrs. Plyler asks: "Can I help you?"

"Just looking," I say in Granny's voice.

The babies must be in the back. Some days they're out front in a big cardboard box, but when it's hot they stay in the back where the fans are. Halfway to the back — about where the arm tattoo kits are — the floor turns from cement to dirt. It gets cooler as you move to the back. And sure enough, there are the babies in their box. Two of them — one red-haired and the other with a headful of golden ringlets.

The golden-haired baby lies on her back and covers her eyes with fists — shy. But the redhead crawls right up to me and makes little noises. I spend a long time just talking to them. The red-haired one hands me up her toys — a squeaky pig, a tinker toy, other stuff. *Mine*, she says if I keep anything too long. I decide to take the redhead, even though the other one is even more beautiful.

And just as I'm about to go up front to pay, the screen door slaps open and Charlie Mae's voice comes down the aisle: "Yes ma'am, yes ma'am, come to fetch...," then she gives my whole name: first, last and middle. Allie must have seen me after all and called Flora.

"She's gone to the back," Mrs. Plyler tells her.

There's no point running. The back door is padlocked. I walk slowly toward Charlie Mae and she begins to fuss over me like a chicken. Out on the street she huffs, "What you think you doing?" When I tell her about buying the baby, she begins to laugh. She can't stop. She totters from the mulberry tree in front of the bank to the

4

mulberry tree in front of the post office. We go past the Spinning Wheel Shop and wave to Allie, then Charlie Mae sits down on the rock wall in front of the Presbyterian Church, bends over double. Now I know what people mean when they say *die laughing*. Charlie Mae will die if she keeps this up. And partly because I don't want her to die and partly because she's laughing at *me*, I begin to cry. Right away Charlie Mae stops. She's got a good heart for one thing, and for another she doesn't want to bring me home crying.

"Get on my back," she says, "and I'll carry you on home."

We gallop the rest of the way.

In the kitchen Charlie Mae tells Flora about the babies. Flora looks sad. Just last week we talked about babies. I told her how I wanted my Mama to have one.

"Better get her a husband first," she'd warned.

Charlie Mae, telling about the babies, begins laughing again.

"Hush up that foolishness," Flora
tells her.

Flora doesn't say anything more but
I can tell she's upset. There's a hen on the
kitchen table — "the old sister." I climb up
on the radiator to watch Flora dress it. I tell
her, "The sign says *Everything That's All*."

"But that don't mean babies. It's
against the law to sell babies."

There's no use arguing with Flora.

She's getting to the exciting part
now, her hand entering the hen cave. It
brings out the egg sac, the liver and the
heart. Then she takes out the craw, slits it
open and scrapes out the sand, washing
away the last of it under the faucet. Finally she separates the eggs and puts them
out on a butter plate.

"Maybe I won't ask my mama for a
baby," I tell Flora. (Mama might get desperate and marry the bootlegger — a widower trying hard to raise three wild

daughters, she told me after I almost bit him on the leg.)

"Best leave well enough alone," says Flora, rolling the bread for stuffing.

Chapter 2

1931

JIMMY WALKER
AND
THE SPINNING WHEEL LOLLIPOPS

After we pull out of the station, I ask Granny, "Where're we going on this bus?"

We were supposed to take an auto-giro to New York City and land on the Flatiron Building, look down and see all the people below. One of those ant people would be waving a handkerchief, and that would be Uncle Eric.

"What about the Flatiron Building?" I ask Granny.

She laughs. "Oh well... that was just my little fairy tale."

"Well, when we gonna eat our lunch?"

"Oh we'll take a little nibble as soon as we cross the Virginia line."

Granny pats my head. She has this way of patting that starts out comforting, then as she gets to thinking about her Spinning Wheel Candies — the marzipan and peanut brittle, chocolate-covered grapefruit peel, roman punches and silver shot, jelly squares and nougat, butterscotch lollipops and chocolate creams — she pats harder and harder until her gold wedding band knocks against my skull and I say *ouch*.

This is going to be a long ride. I fix my mind on the silver dollar Dr. Ted Wallace gave me yesterday. Ted Wallace is a professor at the University who's written a lot of books and gone lots of places like Denmark and China and Iraq and written about the schools over there. Anyway, he came over to our house all serious-faced and took me into the dining room. "Now Mariah," he said, "when you get to New York, I want you to look up a young friend of mine. His name is Jimmy Walker. Can you remember that?"

"Jimmy Walker."

"Now I want you to get in touch with Jimmy Walker"—he put the silver dollar in my hand—"and I want the two of you to go to the Bronx Zoo and after you've seen all the animals, have a special treat."

"How old is Jimmy Walker?"

"Older than you," is what Ted Wallace said, "but not much older. Not much older at all."

I figure my Uncle Eric will know how to find Jimmy Walker. I'll ask him soon as we get to New York City. If we ever do on this slow old bus.

After we cross the Virginia line, Granny gives me a beaten biscuit, a deviled egg and a rabbit lollipop, and I go to sleep. She wakes me to eat the rest of the lunch, then later to see the Washington Monument and the dome of the Capitol. The next time she wakes me up, she's waving out the window, and there is Uncle Eric in his straw hat pushed back the way she hates it and his coat off and suspenders showing — a sight she can hardly bear to see. He's smiling and as soon as he sees my head at the window, he makes his wampus face and does his wampus shuffle so that the people waiting for buses stare at him. "Eric," my grandmother calls, "*please.*"

"Uncle Eric," I shout and hold up six fingers. "I'm six now."

"It's little, it's little, it's little," is his answer.

Uncle Eric lives right off Columbus Avenue at 71st Street, on the fourth floor, but he walks up because he doesn't trust elevators. Granny and I ride. We will sleep in his room and he will sleep on a cot in the hall. The other people who live in this apartment are named Fermini. They say we can use the kitchen after they finish their dinner. We have potato salad, poppy seed rolls, salami, and baked beans. Uncle Eric bought it all from the delicatessen on Columbus Avenue. Granny thinks it's not a very well-balanced meal. "Tomorrow we'll go to the automat," Uncle Eric promises.

"Uncle Eric, do you know Jimmy Walker?" I ask when we're eating the ice cream.

"The little thing wants to know about Jimmy Walker," he says.

Granny sits up straight. "Eric, do answer the child sensibly."

"I saw Jimmy Walker just the other day," Uncle Eric says, "leading a parade."

What is he, I wonder — a boy king?

In the largest of Granny's string bags there's a box of lollipops I packed myself. For Jimmy Walker. None of the little-kid lollipops — acorns and cornucopias and kewpies and strawberries. This box is full of big-kid lollipops — tennis rackets and ponies and two kinds of rabbits, one on its haunches, the other leaning against an

Easter egg.

In Uncle Eric's room my head is next to the elevator shaft, so it's late before I get to sleep. But it works out all right because long after Granny is snoring away beside me, I'm wide awake, and after I'm sure she won't "rise up out of the toils of sleep," I get up and sneak out her string bag with Jimmy Walker's lollipops. I slip off the gold twine and lift the box top, fold back the eyelet paper, take off the quilted cover and the layer of waxed paper and pick a red rabbit on its haunches to take over to the window. It's September and still hot. The view from Uncle Eric's window is the apartment house next door. You can look right into the people's windows and they can look back into yours. There's a boy about my age looking out his window one floor down. I stare at him a long time but he doesn't look up. I bite down on the rabbit's ear. It shatters against my teeth like glass.

The next morning we go to the

automat. Uncle Eric has taken three days of his vacation to show us around the city. At the automat we find the coffee lions Granny promised, but I thought they'd be much bigger and maybe even roaring. I ask for coffee milk just to see it come pouring out of the lion's mouth. At another automat, coffee comes out of dolphins' mouths, but I like the lions better. Later we see real lions at the Bronx Zoo, but Jimmy Walker doesn't meet us there.

Granny stops to study the candy displays in every show window and sometimes goes in the store and buys a box, "to see what the competition is doing." Whenever she eats a piece of candy she holds her nose high and closes her eyes. "They wax their chocolate creams," she says, or "too strong on the roman punch." Back at Uncle Eric's apartment, she makes caramels for us and the Ferminis. After she cuts each wedge she holds it up to light, "to test its purity."

Our third day in New York Uncle Eric buys me a sea horse at the aquarium, but I lose it at the Roxy. Uncle Eric goes all the way back to the aquarium and buys me another one. "I hate to see the little thing cry," he tells Granny.

Jimmy Walker is down to six lollipops now. I've eaten mostly rabbits, but last night I had to eat one green tennis racket.

The little boy on the floor below hasn't looked up yet. And day after tomorrow we have to leave for home because my school is starting.

Back home again, things seem pretty boring after New York. Then one day Ted Wallace's daughter Kate asks me to go to a movie with her. Kate is older than me but sometimes she takes me places. The Pathe news is on when we walk into the Pickwick Theatre, and I hear the announcer say *Jimmy Walker*. "Where's Jimmy Walker?" I ask Kate.

"The one leading the parade."

A man who looks like a dancer steps along, millions of people following him. Well, thousands. He tips his derby hat to someone in the crowd.

"That *man* is Jimmy Walker?" I ask Kate.

"Well who did you think?"

Who did I think? I thought, a boy with hair to his shoulders, like a prince's. I thought, riding in a chariot drawn by horses or even lions. But I won't tell Kate I thought these things.

The very next week Granny tells me she's going to pass along the secrets of her trade to me, but not all at once. First I have to learn to wash my hands clear up to the elbows. Then I'll sit on a stool at one of the high counters and separate the fluted candy cups — brown for chocolate, white for bon bons. Last I put pecan halves on top of the chocolate creams.

The Presidential Candidates

Franklin D. Roosevelt
Democrat

Herbert Hoover
Republican

ROOSEVELT — HOOVER
PRESIDENTIAL SCORE SHEET
HOURLY TREND—NOVEMBER 8TH, 1932
7 P. M. TO MIDNIGHT

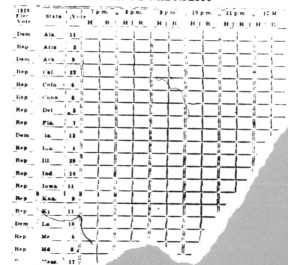

1928 Elec. Vote	State	Vote	7 p.m.		8 p.m.		9 p.m.		10 p.m.		11 p.m.		12 M	
			H	R	H	R	H	R	H	R	H	R	H	R
Dem	Ala.	11												
Rep	Aris	3												
Dem	Ark.	9												
Rep	Cal.	22												
Rep	Colo.	6												
Rep	Conn.	8												
Rep	Del.	3												
Rep	Fla.	7												
Dem	Ja.	13												
Rep	Ida.	4												
Rep	Ill.	29												
Rep	Ind.	14												
Rep	Iowa	11												
Rep	Kan.	9												
Rep	Ky.	11												
Dem	La.	10												
Rep	Me	5												
Rep	Md	8												
	Mass.	17												

Chapter 3

1932

THE STRANGE WAYS
OF
DEMOCRACY

I'm waiting for my mama at the polls.
It's really the firehouse and police station
and stands right in the middle of University Avenue. On the second floor is the
jailhouse, where I had to go once when
Millicent Manley and I were pestered at the

Meeting of the Waters by some foreign man who maybe just didn't understand American ways and how it wasn't a good idea to ask two grammar school girls to go for a walk in the woods. And when Mr. Manley took us to the police station to identify the man after they picked him up, we went up the stairs to the jail and there he was in a little cage barely big enough for him to prop himself up on his elbow. And while Millicent was saying, Yes, that's him all right, and told how he lifted her up and how he wouldn't stop laughing, I kept wanting to scream, Just let him out! Which they finally did and then deported him.

Anyhow. This same building that stands smack in the middle of University Avenue is where people come today to vote for Mr. Hoover or Mr. Roosevelt and also for a bunch of county people like judges.

Everyone in this town is a Democrat except us. And we are Republicans for the dumbest reason. When Granny got married, she and her husband made a bargain. She would become a Republican like him if he would become a Presbyterian like her. He was a Baptist and she was a Democrat. I guess maybe religion meant more to her than politics back in those days. Anyway, that's how it happened. If she'd agreed to be a Baptist and he'd agreed to be a Democrat, I'd be a lot happier today. I'm the only one in my entire school whose family is Republican, and I'm tired of having people make fun of me. Besides, I think Mr. Hoover's made a mess of things. "Mr. Roosevelt may be our only hope," Flora said yesterday to her daughter Bernice, and Flora's a Republican herself because Mr. Lincoln freed the slaves and her daddy was a slave. But she doesn't vote, even though she can read and write and knows all kinds of stories. My favorite is the one about Mother Ceres, Proserpine, Mr. Pluto and the Underworld.

Anyway. Mama doesn't know I'm waiting here. I heard her tell Granny this morning that she was going to vote on her lunch hour. So I've come on my lunch hour too, to persuade her to vote for Mr. Roosevelt.

And here she comes, just strolling along. It always makes me happy to see her. Even today, when I know she's planning to vote for gloomy old Mr. Hoover and not for Mr. Roosevelt who's out to save America.

She has on the pin with Mother spelled out in periwinkle shells that I made in summer crafts shop. The other mothers said, Oh how nice, and put theirs away in the bottom of their jewelry boxes. But my mama wears hers, sometimes two days in a row. In her wedding pictures she looks just like a movie star. But now she's gotten a little stout, and her hair is parted in the middle and pulled straight back in a bun.

And she has to wear glasses. She's been a widow lady since she was twenty-three and I was one day old.

She has the nicest voice. Right now it's saying to me, "Well, hello, Babe, and what are *you* doing here?" and I'm trying not to smile at her so she'll know how serious I take this voting business.

"Mama, I've come down to beg you one more time to vote for Mr. Roosevelt."

"Well, honey, Mr. Roosevelt is a Democrat, and I'm a registered Republican. My *papa* was a Republican."

"On Granny's side, you're a Democrat."

"That's true."

One thing I'll have to say for my mama is, she's always fair. It makes it hard to win an argument with her. But I'm going to try. I remind her of the bargain Granny made with her husband that changed us into Republicans and tell her I think it's silly to be sticking to that bargain today. I tell her that Mr. Hoover has almost wrecked this country and that Mr. Roosevelt is going to save it.

"Well, when you get old enough to vote, you can vote for whomever you choose," she says in her pleasant voice. "I'll certainly not tell *you* how to vote."

"But it's because I can't vote that I want you to vote for Mr. Roosevelt."

She shakes her head a little and looks up at the town clock. Quarter past twelve.

I remind her that Uncle Eric lost his bank job in New York and has been living in our basement room ever since. I remind her that Granny's Spinning Wheel Shop may go under because of the sorry state the country is in. And finally I remind her that the University had to cut her salary because they were short of money.

"True enough," she says.

She's smoking a Camel. Last week she asked me if I thought she should give up smoking, and I said, "No, Mama, it's your one pleasure in life." I heard her telling her friends what I'd said when they came for cocktails Saturday. All her friends are Democrats. And they were arguing with her, just like I am now. I look her straight in the eye. "Mama, don't you want me to grow up in a democracy?"

She looks down, takes one last puff on her Camel, then crushes it out with the toe of her left shoe. She takes forever to crush out a cigarette — never gives a spark a chance. This time it takes her longer than usual. I study her face. She's doing her mouth a funny way, trying not to laugh or trying not to cry, I can't tell which.

Finally she looks at me. "Well, Babe, I'm gonna keep in mind all you've said. And yes, I certainly do want you to grow up in a democracy. Here in this country we have what we call the secret ballot, and when you walk into that polling booth, your vote is between yourself and the ballot you mark. You don't have to tell anyone how you vote. So you remember that when you cast *your* first ballot."

She starts into the firehouse, then turns to say, "Why don't you park your bike and come in with me. Then after I vote, we can go get something scrumptious to eat."

The polling booths are tiny little closets with curtains across the front. Mama's legs show at the bottom. I know she's voting for Mr. Hoover, but somehow I'm not mad at her anymore. She turns but doesn't come back out. She may be counting her money to see if we have to go some place where she can charge or whether we can pay cash. She never knows which it'll be — cash or charge. When I grow up and begin making money, I'll treat her every single time.

She draws back the curtain and comes out, goes over to the table where a lady and gentleman are sitting with a big box between them. Carefully Mama slides her ballots into the slot.

Chapter 4

1934

THE COLORS OF BONBONS,
THE DARK OF CHOCOLATE CREAMS

After the Spinning Wheel Shop closed down, Granny kept right on "plying her trade" and moved her candy kitchen to the basement of our house. Not basement like the furnace room is basement, with red dirt piled behind cement walls — the candy room is clean and white, with windows running clear down to the floor and white tie-back curtains. And it has a little bathroom, where I have to scrub my hands clear up to the elbows every time I help out in the candy-making. Scrub with the brown soap Flora and Granny make outdoors in a black kettle.

Uncle Eric had been staying down in this basement room with all his newspapers and big-eraser pencils and rubberbands and paper clips and note pads and his two good suits hanging from the overhead pipe. The pants to these suits each has a pie-slice of a different material sewed in at the back, because his "mid-section is expanding," as Granny says. My midsection is expanding too, what with all the candy I eat. More than anyone knows, tell the truth. Anyway, Uncle Eric had to move to the attic where he can stay till the weather turns hot, but before that he hopes to go back to New York to find "suitable employment,"as Granny says. Times will get better, she's certain of that.

Before she opened the Spinning Wheel Shop, Granny studied at the Candy Institute in New York City. Mrs. Callah, who ran the Institute, always warned her students, "Never wax your chocolates." "Waxing" means putting paraffin in the melted chocolate before you dip the centers, to give the chocolates a gleam. But the paraffin leaves a "waxy residue" in the mouth, Granny says, and sure enough, I can taste it whenever I eat pieces of drugstore candy.

Another thing Mrs. Callah used to say was, "Reveal your trade secrets to only one person." *I* am Granny's chosen person. Next year, when I'm ten, I'll become the "official Spinning Wheel Candies apprentice." Not even Allie, who Granny says can dip a bonbon as neat as Mrs. Callah herself, knows all the secrets. Neither does Mama or Granny Grand. Just me. Or rather I'll know them one day. In the meantime, Granny says I am to "watch and listen and learn."

Sometimes she reads from Mrs. Callah's *Guide to Fine Candy-making*. "Knowledge is Earning Power" is on its cover — gold letters. Yesterday I learned that candy made on rainy days will be sticky and that you need to cook hard candies fast because slow cooking makes them cloudy.

"Fondant is the foundation of all cream candies," Mrs. Callah says. You use it for bonbon centers and chocolate cream centers too. To make the fondant you put cream, sugar, and salt in a kettle and stir until they make a syrup. You cook this syrup until the candy thermometer reads 240 degrees, then pour it out on a piece of marble that has slab irons around the top to keep the fondant from running off. You take the fondant creamer (it looks like a putty knife) and work the syrup back and forth from outside to center. At first the fondant is the no-color of milky water and about as thick as waffle batter. Then as Granny creams it ("until you cannot cream it any more," Mrs. Callah says), it gets stiffer and whiter until it turns into fondant.

Next you divide it into small loaves, which you put in a crock and let "ripen" for twenty-four hours. Then you flavor them. Like if you want to make a batch of pistachio creams, you color the fondant light green and add flavoring. Or for orange bonbons you use the orange flavoring and cut up little pieces of crystallized orange peel, then dip the centers in orange fondant re-melted in a double boiler.

You have to color the bonbon icing very carefully. As Mrs. Callah says: "It is well to remember in using coloring, that more can be added if necessary, but if used too heavily, it is too late to remove it." Granny says the bonbons must be "muted" and not look like eggs dyed by children who love Easter-chick yellow and grass-green and pink halfway to red. And when you dip the centers in the icing, you twist the dipping fork around to make a little coil on top of each bonbon.

And all kinds of chocolate creams are made from the fondant too: vanilla, raspberry, roman punch, pistachio, chocolate nut, almond, and lots more. Some are covered in milk chocolate, which tastes the best and some are covered in bittersweet, which looks the most beautiful. Some kinds of chocolate creams you roll in chocolate shot or ground nut meats. I guess I'd have to say the vanilla chocolate creams are my favorite. They're big, for one thing, and that dark chocolate over the pure white fondant is the most beautiful sight you could ever hope to see. And there's a pecan half on top.

On Sunday afternoons when the grown-ups are resting, or sometimes in the evening when Mama's gone out and the grannies are listening to Phil Spitalny and his All-Girl Orchestra or one of their other radio programs, I slip down to the candy room and have a prowl around. But first I wash my hands with brown soap.

What I do mostly is just harmless stuff like snip off a few inches of ribbonzine and gold tinsel cord. Or I test the black rubber mats that mold the heart-shaped mints, to make sure they're not cracked anywhere. And I might stack up the miniature hat boxes we pack the Easter candy in, or check the bottles of coloring to be sure their labels are turned to the front. Atlas Food Colors are what we use. Dependable Since 1851. Hercules red, velvetine black, goldine orange, ice cream biscuit shade, emeraldine green, and lots of others.

On my prowls, I'll sometimes sneak a piece or two of candy, but mostly from the "ugly tray" at the bottom of the showcase — a vanilla cream with a broken pecan half. Or some mint crumbles or a streaked bonbon or lop-sided roman punch. Some of the guava jelly squares show through the chocolate, and I'll take a couple of those. I try never to take anything that Granny could sell.

But one night I go a little wild. I grab up one of the Easter hat boxes that has a "blemish," one Granny will use for a close friend who's not paying, and begin packing it with everything in sight. And not from the ugly tray either. Three opera caramels — vanilla cream, chocolate, and raspberry — then a marzipan carrot, a piece of French nougat and a piece of Turkish paste. Three pieces of peanut brittle, a French mocha rolled in ground pecans, two pieces of marshmallow velvet fudge. And several bonbons and chocolate creams.

And now the Easter hatbox is so full I can't get the top on, let alone tie the ribbon, so I put two thicknesses of cellophane over the top and "secure" it with a rubber band. I latch up the show case, close the door to the candy room, and start up the stairs.

Midway up, the steps bend sharp right, and when I make that turn, I see Granny waiting for me.

At my house there aren't any whippings. Just one time Granny switched me when Mary Lou Rowland and me dug up Ted White's periwinkle and transplanted it to my sandpile. So here is how I get punished for stealing candy. Mama sits me down and tells me how hard Granny works and how much effort she puts into this candy business. How good Granny is to me and how she's teaching me her trade. And she ends the lecture with: "And, Babe, you just cannot eat up the profits of our family business." And then Granny says: "With great regret, I must deny you entry to the candy room for two weeks."

So for several days I feel just awful — a disgrace to the family name. To *all* the family names — Thorne, Greenlea, and MacLean.

Then Uncle Top comes up from Florida to visit Granny Grand, and one night at the supper table he says to Granny: "Brownie, you remember how you used to raid the sugar bowl?" He turns to me. "Your grandmother would take five or six spoonfuls, one right after the other."

Granny sighs. "The curse of the Irish, Top. If I'd been a man, I'd have been a drinking man."

"Well, you sure took that sugar mighty neat." Uncle Top laughs his belly laugh.

So *I* must have the curse of the Irish too.

"Well, you just have to learn to control the urge," Granny says. "With candy and liquor both."

"Brownie's got a strong character," Uncle Top says.

"Indeed she has," Granny Grand agrees.

"And I do too," I say. "Or *will* have,

one of these days."

They all laugh and Granny lets me slice the pecan pie.

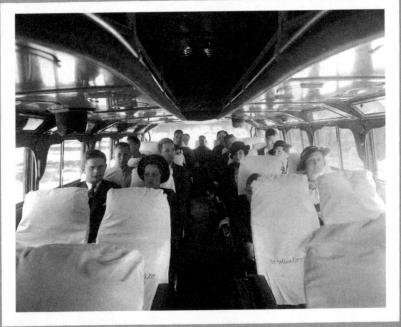

Chapter 5

1935

PLESSY VS. FERGUSON

We're coming down the mountain, Granny and me, bringing my cousin Lolly back with us. She's got long golden hair, curly, and see-through blue eyes. And she's growing bosoms and yawns a lot when we play paper dolls now. Boys are beginning to look at her. The bus driver took a lot of time putting her hat box on the overhead rack.

I wish we'd come by train. On a train

you go through tunnels, and if there are enough cars you can look down and see the caboose winding below. And boys and girls come out on their back porches to wave handkerchiefs. Nothing to do on a bus. I'm too old to kick the seat in front of me, and besides, this time it's the driver's seat.

ERNEST TURNER
Safe Reliable Courteous

his sign reads.

Lolly got the window seat because she's "the little company." I didn't know you were company unless you were inside a house. She doesn't want to play cow poker, so I sing, "May I Sleep in Your Barn To-night, Mister?" under my breath.

There's a lot of colored people at the back, a few laughing but not real loud. Mr. Ernest Turner, Safe, Reliable, Courteous, calls back, "Quiet, you people back there!" Across the aisle Granny jumps, and her

42

face starts ticking in one steady spot. That bus driver better watch out, is all I can say.

When we pull into the Roxville station, a crowd stands waiting, whites in front, colored people behind, about the same number of each. There's too many people unless a lot of riders get off here. Only four do, one a baby who sat in her mama's lap the whole way. So there's three seats. I count the people outside — thirty!

"All right, you people, you'll have to get off here," Mr. Courteous Reliable Turner shouts.

"Which peoples you mean?" a man in back calls out.

"You know who I mean. All you colored people." He pronounces that word *cullud*.

There's a lot of rustling at the back and a slow procession starts to the front. Then everyone stops. "Move on," calls out the same voice that had asked the question *who.* "We gotta move on."

What's the matter? I turn to check with Granny but she's not in her seat. The driver's standing at the top of the steps, stopped. Then I see why — Granny's blocking the way. She's not much taller than me, but she's not going to let Mr. Turner off, or the colored people behind him either. The colored people wait with their bundles and babies, pretending not to notice what's happening. I think I know who's going to win this battle.

"Sir," Granny says, "let me ask you something. Are you acquainted with Plessy Versus Ferguson?" The driver says the name over three times. It's like he knows that last name — lots of Fergusons around, but those first and middle names have him stumped. Besides, he has urgent business and this isn't the time to discuss somebody he doesn't even know. Still he is courteous — reliable too. So he waits.

Granny goes on: "Plessy Versus

44

Ferguson is a decision of the Supreme Court of the United States."

The back of Mr. Turner's neck gets red. You can tell he's a man willing to pick up knowledge any way he can. But right now he has to move one set of people off this bus and get another set on. He steps a foot closer to my grandmother.

"According to Plessy Versus Ferguson," she goes on, "white people sit from the front to the middle, colored people from the middle to the back. Plessy Versus Ferguson is the law of our land."

That bus driver better give up. I've been stopped going up or down the stairs at home, and I always have to do what she says, stubborn as I am.

Granny says: "You look like a nice young man, and I would hate to have to report you to the authorities."

I can see that my grandmother has got to Mr. Turner. Not frightened him or touched his heart, but he sees what I could have told him all along — if you want to get on with your own business, you'd better first do what Granny says.

He pulls up a long sigh and turns to the colored people. "You folks go on back to your seats. Go all the way to the back."

He sounds almost kind. He leaves the bus and Granny slips back into her seat. "Folks, I can't put but six of you on," the driver's voice floats back into the bus, "and some of those will have to stand. But I'll get the ticket agent to call over to Reynolds and send another bus. Best I can do." He lets on six old folks, two of them colored. He punches the new tickets, then swings himself in and slides into his seat, not looking at my grandmother.

No one is speaking to her. The white people are mad: I hear them muttering *of all the nerve* and things like that. And the colored people can't speak to her because they're too far back. So it's up to me. I stare at her hard till she looks over, then hold up two fingers stuck together. She holds up her two. Our signal, meaning two good friends. Nothing can come between us.

I look over at Lolly. At first I think she's watching the scenery, but then I see she's admiring her face in the mirror the window makes. What I wouldn't give to have her eyes. Like marbles that you hold up to light and admire the color. When I lean forward and stare at her, side view, I can see through her eyeballs to the moving trees. If I had just one of her eyes, Hobart Wallace, fifth-grade marble champ, would give me double the price of his best agate for it.

M-O-T-H-E-R
(A WORD THAT MEANS THE WORLD TO ME)

Lyric by
HOWARD JOHNSON

Music by
THEODORE MORSE

Slowly, with expression

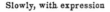

"M" is for the mil-lion things she gave me,

"O" means on-ly that she's grow-ing old,

"T" is for the tears were shed to save me,

"H" is for her heart of pur-est gold, _____

Arr. by Hugo Frey

7767-2

Chapter 6

1935

M IS FOR THE MILLION THINGS
I GAVE HER

Sunday after next is Mother's Day. Usually I make my mama a present, not buy one. When I was little I never ran out of ideas. One year I made her a stegosaurus out of plaster of Paris and it still sits on her desk at the office, crushing down a stack of papers. Next I started cross-stitching a gold cat on a black satin background. I gave it to her Mother's Day before last when I'd only done the outline and the ears and one eye. Then I gave it to her again on her birthday, when I'd done the red bow and the other eye, which is a darker shade of green because I couldn't match the thread I'd started out with. So at Christmas I wrapped it up again. By then it had a plume tail and two front legs. The back legs and most of the gold body were still missing. Then last year for Mother's Day I gave her the whole cat, which Granny sewed on a sofa pillow. Every time I gave Mama the gold cat she'd say, "Why, it's perfectly beautiful," just like I'd never given it to her before.

And there were a lot more gifts I made her, and she wore or used them all, or else put them on the mantelpiece. But this year I can't think of one thing to make her. I may have to buy her some dumb old thing like a pair of stockings. I've looked in the Sears Roebuck catalogue, and my first choice is Ginger Rogers up-to-the-knee silk stockings for 33 cents a pair, but I'm wondering if I should get the outsizes for stout women, 3 pair for 85 cents.

She really is a good mama. But she makes me toe the line. Like Sundays, when all the other kids are whooping it up down in the hollow, swinging on ropes over the chasm, I have to practice my violin exercises. I'll be standing there with tears rolling down my face and she'll be sitting at the piano sounding out the chords. "Just two more exercises," she'll say, "and then you can go out."

She never lets me get by with "clooking." That word comes from one time when I copied down a sentence wrong. I was supposed to write: Which clock says six o'clock? but what I wrote was: Witch clook says six o'clook? Ever since then, Mama has called making silly mistakes "clooking." She'll read my papers and circle the errors, then say, "Watch the clooking, Babe."

But I'm getting a lot better. I might even write her a little book of poems for Mother's Day.

When I grow up I'm going to buy my mama a whole new wardrobe like the trousseau Granny bought her at Garfinkel's in Washington, D. C. When you're a widow you have to spend your money on other things, which is why Mama is always making something over, usually a hand-me-down from a stylish cousin.

I don't know why Mama's stayed a widow all these years. Dozens of men have wanted to marry her — well, three or four for sure. But she turns up her nose at all of them.

"It is the central mystery of my life," Granny said to Granny Grand the other day, "why she does not remarry."

It is the central mystery of my life too.

One time when the writer Thomas

Wolfe was in town, some friends had Mama over to dinner with him. He seemed to take a shine to her and asked if he could call her the next evening. She wrote down her phone number for him.

When Mama told us about all this, I asked, "What's this Tom Wolfe like, anyway?"

"To tell the truth, he's like a giant little boy," Mama said.

"Exactly what do you mean?" Granny asked.

"Well, he calls his mother and father Mama and Papa."

"There's nothing wrong with that," Granny said. "You always called your papa Papa and me Mama. To this very day, as a matter of fact."

"Oh around home, of course." Mama lit up a Camel. "But out in public, I'd refer to you as 'my father and mother.' I wouldn't say, 'Back when Papa was a boy,' or 'Mama used to say.'.. the way he does."

"Well, I think it's nice and informal, calling your parents Mama and Papa."

Granny has this way of looking off into space like her eye is gazing at the hills of home.

"Well, he probably won't call," Mama said.

The next evening we all waited for the phone to ring with Tom Wolfe's voice at the other end. When it finally did, it was Mama's friend Jenny Curtis asking her to go see "It Happened One Night." And Mama accepted. Granny and I argued with her, but she was determined. "I tell you, he won't call." And she counted the money in her pocketbook.

And he didn't call. Did he lose her phone number? Did he suddenly have to go back to New York? Or did he know she wouldn't be there waiting for his call? Mama was too proud to ask *why?* to the friend who'd had her to dinner with him. And to tell the truth, she didn't really care all that much anyway.

Now it's only two more days till Mother's Day, and I'm getting pretty desperate. It's too late to order the Ginger Rogers knee-length stockings or the stout size either. But I'll go down to Plyler's Five and Dime and let Mrs. Plyler help me find something "suitable." An I'm making Mama something too. Uncle Top sent Granny Grand a record of himself singing some songs. The last song was "M-O-T-H-E-R," and the words go like this:

M is for the million things she gave me

O means that she's simply growing old

T is for the tears she's shed to save me

H is for her heart of purest gold.

E is for her eyes with love light shining

R is right and right she'll always be.

Put them all together, they spell MOTHER

— A word that means the world to me.

I played Uncle Top's record over and over until I got all the words written down, and now I'm going to print them out nice, with giant letters spelling out MOTHER down the side. Then I'll decorate them. Two fairies are going to be looking through the O and an elf leaning his chin on the E, and like that. But one thing bothers me — though the printing looks good and the letters are really going to be beautiful, these words aren't mine. So I'll write her a poem too. She'll have three things for Mother's Day, but I bet her favorite will be my poem. So here goes —

On Sunday is our
Mother's Day
And I can wear a
red rose I am very
proud to say.
For Mother dear I love
you so, And more and
more as while I grow.
I don't think there could be
near as sweet a mother
as you,
I love you so I really
do

to   mother

Chapter 7

1936-37

RED ROVER   RED ROVER

They're calling my name, but I'm not moving. Maybe if I just stand here looking over at the kudzu jungle, they'll give up and call someone else.

Red Rover Red Rover
Let Mariah come over

"Go on, Mariah," Mary Lou whispers. "You can't just stand there all day."

The voices from the other end of the field get louder, and I can hear Kinley Rich's rising above the rest. I know one thing — I won't try to break through the line at *him*. He has this way of socking you hard in the stomach when you try to, but the substitute teacher we have never calls him down. I think she's afraid of Kinley.

Red Rover Red Rover
Let Mariah come over

Mary Lou drops my right hand. Jon Jocher lets go of my left. Then the two of them join hands. Now I've got to run over to the line facing ours and try to break through that chain of hands. I start a slow trot, working up speed.

Mariah can't break through
an egg cheese sandwich!

Kinley Rich sends that message down his line. They all get silly smiles on their faces, and some start giggling. "An egg cheese sandwich!" Teeny Sparrow collapses, has to get out of line and go sit on the bank to laugh herself out.

My legs have slowed almost to a stop. I notice Junior Martindale standing there with his stick arms. Nell Lloyd holds his left hand. She's frail and wispy. It should be easy to break through the line at those two. And now I start to run again, hard, working up steam. Nell gives me a horrified look. Junior's huge blue eyes get even bigger. He looks like he might cry. Still, he's proud — he'll hold out long as he can. But Nell lets go before I even touch her. She shakes her wrist, bends her shoulders, like I've hurt her bad. Nobody saw what happened except me and Junior, so everyone thinks I've broken through fair and square. From across the playground my team sends up a weak cheer. And now

Kinley Rich shouts,

> Junior Martindale can't
> hold back a broken-tail cat!

I look down the line to Kinley. How can he be so handsome and so mean at the same time? Black curly hair, red-red lips, a little moustache already sprouting. He's two years older than the rest of us — failed two grades. Granny says Kinley's father is as queer as Dick's hatband. Never speaks when he passes you downtown. Kinley's mother is dead. They live miles out the Sparrow's Ferry Road. Sometimes Kinley rides into town on a brown mule, but no one would dare tease him or feel sorry for him, unless that person wanted a bloody nose.

"So take one of 'em and go on back to where you came from," Kinley shouts. He's mad because I've been staring at him.

Nell's still shaking her arm like it will never be the same. What a coward!

But Junior, even though his eyes look hurt, is being brave.

"Come on, Junior," I say and take hold of his sweater.

He pries open my fingers and tosses my hand away, then smooths out the sweater where I grabbed it.

"Go on," he says. "I'll follow."

"I'm sorry, Junior." Sorry for all the things I've done to him during this recess, but mostly for Kinley Rich's teasing. I smile , hoping he'll smile back. But he looks down at the ground. I can see he's never going to forgive me.

Mary Lou and Jon Jocher won't let me back in line, so I have to go to the end, take Buddy Meacham's fat hand. Our team calls Teddy Oliver from the other side, and he breaks through Mary Lou and Jon. Takes Jon back with him. When I see Mary Lou look like she's about to cry, my hurt feelings go away. I'm happy she's unhappy. That's the trouble with Red Rover — it makes me hate everyone. Friend and foe alike, as Granny says.

Then Kinley Rich starts the call for Coreen Cheek to come over. She huffs onto the field and — crazy girl — heads straight for Kinley and Wallace Petrie, another bully. She hangs over their two arms, shuffling her feet. Still they hold the line. I see Kinley give her a stomach sock, but not as hard as he's done to others. So she has to give up and get in that line. She takes Kinley Rich's hand. I wonder, was that what she wanted anyhow? She doesn't look too unhappy.

And now the bell rings. One more day I've lived through Red Rover.

The next day is Friday. I wake up with an upset stomach. "Better go on to school," Mama says as she leaves for work. But Granny says, "Midge, let her rest up till Monday." So I do, and even though Mama makes me stay home from the Sunday movie since I was too sick to go to school, it was worth it to have a day off.

And by Monday everything's changed. Our regular teacher Miss York is back for one thing, and though she's real strict and sometimes mean, she doesn't put up with anything from Kinley Rich. We've just taken off our coats when she shakes him by the shoulders until his hair falls in his eyes. She's shouting, "You better listen to me, young man, or you're going to wish you had."

At recess, instead of lining us girls up for Red Rover, Miss York takes us over to the bank and sits us down to play Gossip. Mr. Mullins, the new principal, comes out in his hat and rounds up the boys, takes them to the edge of the kudzu jungle and drills them, like they were in the Army. Going in from recess, I find out that on Friday Kinley Rich broke Jon Jocher's wrist in Red Rover, so we're not going to be playing *that* game any more. Back in the classroom, Miss York and Kinley have another set-to, and he goes to his desk and puts his head down till lunch time. I feel kind of sorry for him, tell the truth.

But all that was back in sixth grade. Now we're in seventh, and we play basketball and softball, separate teams for boys and girls.

I'm working on one little specialty in each game — I never strike out in softball and never lose the ball in basketball. Sometimes when the best softball players are worn out someone will call, "Put old Mariah in. She never strikes out!"

"And she never hits a home run neither" — Coreen Cheek, but what do I care about her? I just step up to the plate and hit those balls, at least far enough to get to first base, sometimes second. Most of the time I get home. Eventually.

And an amazing thing happened on

the basketball court the other day. I had the ball, with Enid Waters and Judith Hudgins guarding me. I'd just taken my third dribble when Catherine Holmes moved past, her skinny legs pumping toward the basket. She raised her eyebrows at me, and I threw the ball high to her. She just tapped it with her fingers, mid-air, and it went right through the hoop.

So naturally everyone was pounding her back and raising her arms, and then she yelled: "But I never cudda done it without Mariah!" And everybody turned to me, and for a few seconds, *I* was in the spotlight.

But I don't think I want to be a star all the time. They pound you on the back too hard, for one thing. And if the others began to expect too much from me, I just might get nervous and lose the ball. I'm better off staying where I am.

The Jones House
That they
Live in
Now

Chapter 8

1936-37

KEEPING UP WITH THE JONESES

During boring old arithmetic class I look across the aisle and see Mary Lou drawing circles around her lunch money. Two circles out of her quarter, four from her nickel, four from her dime, and four from one of her pennies. She looks up and signals something — I can't make out what. Maybe she's got extra money and is willing to treat.

By recess her money circles have

become faces — mama and papa faces, four girl faces, four boy faces, and four baby faces. "It's a family," she explains. "We're gonna write a book about them."

"Why?" I want to know.

Don't we have enough to do already? Miss York makes us write all the time. Stories, poems, plays. She thinks sixth graders can write anything. And now here is Mary Lou, thinking we can write a whole book.

"Well how nice!" Mary Lou's mother says when we tell her what we're up to. She lets us go in Mr. Rowland's study and even lights the fire in the fireplace and makes us cocoa. So we've got to do it. First we make bodies to go with the heads. We draw a house and car, some other stuff.

"We better get down to the writing," Mary Lou says when I start on more pictures. "We'll illustrate as we go along."

She dictates for awhile and I write, then we swap. Sometimes one of us interrupts to give a better word or a funnier line. Sometimes we have to stop and laugh.

"This is a real collaboration," Mary Lou's mother says when she comes in with cookies.

It's not often you can make a mother this happy.

"Thank you, Mrs. Rowland," I say, remembering my manners but taking the biggest cookie. Writing really makes you hungry.

By the time I have to go home, we have Chapter I finished. We read it over:

The Jones Family live in a little two-story house on a hill in the town of Melisse. In the family is a mother and a Pa. Four girls, four boys, and four babies. The girls are the oldest their names are Julia, Jane, Jenny, and Jean.

The boys are next. Their
names are Jack, Jim, John,
and Jerry. The babies are the
youngest, their names are Bob,
Ben, Bruce and Bill.

They also have a cook, and
two maids. The cook's name
is Hannah. The maid's names
are Tilda and Lizzie. They have
two maids because one waits on
the table when only the family
is there. They do this because
Lizzie <u>couldn't</u> wait on the table
when guests were there because
she is always chewing chewing gum.

When the Jones go any-
where they go in their little blue
auto. The mother and all the
girls get in the back. Each girl
holds a baby. All the boys get in
the front with Pa. Pa is very
proud of the little blue auto even

if it is a 1928 model.

The girls wear dresses alike
and so do the boys. The Jones babies wear dresses differnt. Bob and
Bill wear dresses alike and
Bruce and Ben wear dresses alike.
The Jones girls are in the 4th
grade and the Jones boys are in
the first grade at school. The
babies of course are only six
months old so they can't go to school.

The Jones children sleep in
a nursery. 12 little beds are
pushed up next to the wall for
them to sleep in.

We're getting a lot done on this book.
But we don't do anything else. Come right
in from school and start work. Never any
time for our Shirley Temple collection. Or
the Dionne quintuplets scrapbook. And we
haven't played Monopoly in ages. But by

the end of the week we have four more
chapters. Chapter II and III are my fa-
vorites:

Chapter II

The Soda Fountain

Mrs. Jones gave Jenny, Jean,
Julia and Jane a quarter a piece to
go up town to have their hair cut.
So they went uptown. As they
walked along they passed by an
ice cream store. Jane said, "Let's
use our money for ice cream sodas,
and cut our own hair." They all
agreed, so they went in.They
each bought ice cream, sodas,
cookies and candy with their
money. They ate until they
could hold no more. So they
went home, slipped in the side
door, and went upstairs. Jean got

the scissors and they went in
the nursery to cut their hair.
Clip, clip, clip, the hair fell to
the floor. First Jean's, then
Jenny's, then Jane's, and last
Julia's. Then they swept the
floor clean. Just then Tilda came
in the room, and said that
their mother had gone to call on
Mrs. Smith, but she would be home
soon. So the girls went out in
the yard to play. When their mother
came home she said, "Why, my
dears, that is the best haircut
you've had in a long time." They
were very much surprised and
Jenny almost fainted.

Chapter III
Pa and Ma

Pa is a sales man. He is
away from home alot. Pa married

ma in 1926. I will tell you this
ma made a very pretty bride.
She wore a bridal dress and carried
a bunch of forget-me-nots.

I guess you wonder how ma
had twelve children in ten years,
but she only expected to have three
children but she had quadruplets
each time. Now in 1936 they have
twelve children.

Pa and ma met in a drug
store. It was love at first
sight for them. So they got in
pa's car, (it wasn't the blue car
another older model) and went
to the church and got married.

Ma and pa lived on Church
street for a long time in a little
cottage. When the stork brought
Jenny, Jane, Jean and Julia
they moved to the little house on
the hill.

We get interrupted sometimes, like when we have a glee club concert or there's a party. Or even when there are several good movies, one right after the other and some good enough to see twice. But Mary Lou always makes us come back to our book. And now summer has come, and it's no time to be working on a book. First there's Camp Red Fern, then Mary Lou takes off to Atlanta and she's barely back before I go to Texas. All summer, it's that same way. But the Sunday before school starts, Mary Lou says, "It's now or never," and we spend the whole day writing on *The Jones Family*. They go to the beach — one place neither of us got to this year.

It was summer and pa wanted to go to the beach. Julia, Jane and the boys wanted to go too. But ma wanted to go to

the mountains. Jenny and Jean
wanted to go to the mountains
too. But John said that the
majority rules. So ma and Jean
and Jenny gave in.

So they packed their beach
clothes and their bathing suits.
The boys had red trunks. The
girls had green bathing suits.

Ma thought it best to rent
a cottage as they were going to
stay all summer. But pa did better than this. He had one <u>built</u>.

The little blue auto was
packed full, and luggage was all
over it. They had to put a trailer
on it too.

We have Ed Dewsberry and his fam-
ily there at the same beach, so that he and
Jenny can continue their romance. Then
Jean meets her ideal man, Otto Honk, and

he is very handsome. Jane and Julia laugh at their sisters for having "beau lovers."

I've been noticing how Mary Lou smiles at boys these days. And she keeps looking at them, smiling, and nodding her head when they talk to her. I bet she wouldn't mind getting a pretend diamond from Jon Jocher, one like Ed Dewsberry gave Jenny in our book.

Anyway. We finish the book at 5:30 that afternoon. It's too late to read the last chapter aloud, so we just put it away in her desk.

And Mary Lou was right. We never would have gone back to it if we hadn't finished it that afternoon. The seventh grade has been moved to the basement and the boys separated from the girls. "Experiment in learning." "Fewer distractions." "That age, you know." We listen to the teacher-talk.

What those school officials don't realize is that when they separate us, we begin to notice each other. There they are, those boys, lined up against the wall waiting for us girls to come out of the science room so they can go in. Four times a day we pass each other like that. They *have* to look at us. We have to look at them. And they're beginning to say things. And whistle.

Just before Christmas we sit down in Mr. Rowland's study to read the last chapter of *The Jones Family*.

Chapter XXXI
Autumn

The air was crisp and chilly. The children wore their coats to school now. The girls had had their fifteenth birthday and the boys were twelve years of age. The babies were learning to talk and say their prayers. Pa was

very proud of his other four sons,
(he had eight.)

Jenny was still in love with
Ed Dewsberry and John had met
a little girl named Ellen Ackens
and he had falled head over heels
in love with her.

The little blue auto had had
a new coat of paint. It was beginning to show its age now, for
every time pa ran it up the hill he
had to put it on in full gear.

Agatha Brown had moved to
Farmsville, but a new girl
named Mary Scott had moved
to town.

One night in late Oct. pa
said, "I think, if you all agree,
that we shall move to Pottashville."
Ma sort of wanted to go but all of
the children disagreed; so that
was settled. "Well," put in ma,
"there is no other place as good as

our house in Melisse, is there
dear. To which they <u>all</u> agreed.

THE END

"What we gonna do with this book?"
I ask Mary Lou.

"Well, we can keep it awhile at my
house, then keep it awhile at yours."

Is that *all* we can do with it now that
we've written it? I look around at Mr.
Rowland's books. *United States Code* —
one whole bookcase, going back to 1900.
Blackstone's *Commentaries*. Lots more thick
books with gold letters. No pictures inside.
I think about my daddy's books, the ones
I'm going to inherit some day. *Shakespeare's Time Scheme*. The collected plays
of George Bernard Shaw. Books that cover
three whole walls and spread across the
mantel.

Last month a chapel speaker talked
to us about libraries. "Of the making of
many books there is no end," he said, or

something like that. Quoting somebody famous, Shakespeare maybe. Anyway. Mary Lou and me have made one more book. It's on notebook paper, with eyelets holding the pages in place. It's not printed or bound or anything. But still it's a pretty good little old book.

So we'll swap it back and forth between her house and mine. And maybe some day one of our children will come across it and say to a brother or sister, "Hey, listen to this!"

About the Year 1780,
a company of young
Irishmen left the Emerald
Isle, and set forth, to seek
their fortunes in the
new country, beyond
the sea.

Chapter 9

1937

GENTLE LADY

When the Yankees came to Fair Meadows, my great-grandmother's plantation, one of them bent down to look into her face and said, "Child, your eyes are as black as seven devils." Today Granny Grand's dark pupils are outlined in pale blue. Her hair, which used to be as black as her eyes, is pure white, parted in the middle and brought back behind her ears, which are large and stick out a little. When she does her tatting and crocheting, writes letters or reads, she puts on huge glasses that make her look like an owl. At home she wears dresses that come down to her ankles and slippers with pom-poms. When she goes out in winter she puts on her lace-up shoes and her black karakul cape and muff. Then she looks quite elegant, but around the house she just looks very neat, like an old but good little girl.

She came to live with us when I was eight and she was seventy-eight, and we've become pretty close, even with the difference in our ages. Our birthdays are only one day apart. Last month I celebrated my twelfth birthday, and the next day she celebrated her eighty-second. All eight of her children brought or sent wonderful presents. Her youngest son Bat shipped a deerskin rug from California that she puts her bare feet on first thing in the morning.

Her grandchildren and great-grand-children all gave her gifts too. Mama's was a large green book with blank pages, with this inscription written on the first page:

My Gentle Lady
I present this book to you with
the hope that you will record
within its pages — at your
leisure and whenever it pleases
you to do so — the memories of
your life, interspersed with re-collections — historical and
anecdotal — of our family; so
that your children and grand-children in years to come may read
in this book many accounts of
history which otherwise might
be lost or forgotten.

The first line Granny Grand put in the

green book reads: "About the year 1780, a company of young Irishmen left the Emerald Isle, and set forth; to seek their fortunes in the new country, beyond the sea."

And that's the first news I'd had that we were part Irish. She talks so much about "your Scottish heritage" that I thought we were pure Scotch. But it turns out that my great-grandfather, Colonel MacLean, Granny Grand's husband, brought the Scottish heritage and she brought an Irish heritage. So there we are. And it will all be written down in the green book.

She's making a map of Fair Meadows, showing where the pansies and forget-me-nots were planted and where the cows were milked. She's drawn the croquet ground and the road to Asheville, the mock orange grove and loom house, the vegetable and flower garden, the gooseberry and raspberry patches and the slave quarters — "where the darkies lived" are the words she used.

An older girl who's just moved down from Massachusetts asked me the other day if I didn't feel funny about my ancestors owning *people*, the way you'd own horses and cows. And though I was mad at first, the more I thought about it, the funnier I felt. But there they are in the green book — slaves — Nancy York and her five children, Aunt Milley and *her* five. There's a cabin with two doors where Aunt Belle lived with her three children and Aunt Sarah lived beside her. Aunt Hannah lived with her two children next to the loom house. A hundred slaves in all.

The households all went by the women's names, but there were men slaves too. Families at Fair Meadows were kept together, none of them separated or sold. Some of the men went off to war with their masters. One went with Granny Grand's father, who had to go hide out in the woods when the Yankees were coming. He was too old to be a soldier, but still he'd have been

89

taken prisoner if he'd stayed at Fair Meadows. He didn't want to leave the family, but Big Mother, Granny Grand's mother, insisted. Safer for him, safer for them, she said.

Mammy Sera lived with her eleven children in a cabin facing the Asheville Road. Granny Grand put a note beside the drawing of this cabin that reads: "Mammy Sera was a <u>princess</u> in Africa and had servants of her own." She was mammy to just Granny Grand. Her sister, my great-great Aunt Marianna, had a different mammy. Mammy Sera was beautiful, with long ringlets and "a graceful carriage." The two mammies taught Granny Grand and her sister to swim by slipping wide pieces of cloth under their middles and holding them up in the water, then slowly letting go of the cloth, so they were paddling by themselves.

It was while they were swimming in Doe Creek one day toward the close of the war that they saw the Yankees coming two by two up the Asheville Road. "Admiration is what I first felt," Granny Grand said, "admiration for the perfect beauty of that blue line." These Yankees were part of Stoneman's Raiders. "The sweet potatoes started from the ground when Stoneman came marching through," the saying went.

Some of the officers were gentlemen, but most of the soldiers were wild, and the stragglers, who followed the Union Army and lived off the land, were wilder still. One soldier hung Granny Grand's Confederate soldier doll from an apple tree and cut off its head with his bayonet. Other bayonets cut the heads off turkeys as they sat on their nests. One of the blue coats found the shroud that old Aunt Lucindy had been saving for her burial, put it on and danced around in it, carrying it with him when he left. Yankee boots trampled the boxwood, and horses were led through the ripening wheat. Pillows were slit open and feathers scattered on top of sorghum. Broken eggs were spread across the kitchen floor. Big Mother couldn't stop the soldiers, but she stood on the front porch to give them a strong sense of her disapproval.

There was no controlling the stragglers, though, because they came after the Army left. They carried off anything they could find, like the few treasures not buried in piano boxes or hidden under the loom house floor. One straggler poked around in the clock on the mantelpiece, thinking there might be jewelry hidden inside, but the clock toppled over and gave him a goose egg on his head.

While Granny Grand writes the family history and draws a family tree and finishes the map of Fair Meadows in the first pages of the green book, I write down the stories she tells me, going from the middle to the back. First I scribble them down on notebook paper, and Mama reads them and circles the "clooking" errors, then

I copy them down in the book. I've told how during the war they boiled parched persimmon seeds to make a coffee drink and gathered rose thorns for pins; how Granny Grand learned to knit on polished straws because they couldn't get knitting needles. I've written about how she stood on the porch waving a little Confederate flag as the regiment commanded by her uncle marched off to war. This regiment carried a flag made from the dresses of Miss Anna and Lily Woodfin and Miss Fanny Patton, all of Asheville.

The day before Granny Grand's Cousin Willie went to war he came to Fair Meadows for dinner and afterwards sat on the porch carving her a tiny banjo. She noticed his sad face. He was shot in his first battle, what Granny Grand calls "Manassas I." His brother saw him fall and carried him off the battlefield to the ambulance, but it was too late to save him.

And there is the story of Cousin Trish

Bobbitt, who came to board at Fair Meadows when she was twelve and went to the plantation school there. When she heard that the Yankees were coming, she rode the four miles to her home in Marion to tell her father and brothers. As she galloped off to warn her menfolk, Confederate soldiers home on leave, the Yankees were already at Fair Meadows, firing their guns into the air.

Granny Grand told me a war story about her future husband, Colonel MacLean, whom she didn't meet until many years later, and here is how I copied it down in the green book:

It was at one of the battles of Virginia, toward the middle of the War between the States. A line of gray was at one end of the battle-field, a line of blue at the other. The two sides were not actually fighting, but at any moment the first shot might be fired. A Confederate volunteer was called for, to carry a message to headquarters asking for reinforcements.

Colonel MacLean volunteered. As he rode out between the lines, a ready target for the enemy, the Yankees began firing. With a flourish he removed his cap and bowed low to the enemy. Cheers went up from both sides. And not another shot was fired.

When Granny Grand spoke that last line, she put down her tatting, leaned toward me, and said slowly, so I would remember: "And not another shot was fired."

Fair Meadows is still standing. But the present owner stores hay in the parlor and rides horses through the boxwood. I can see how it hurts Granny Grand to have the old home place treated like this. What

I want to do when I get rich is buy back Fair Meadows and give her the deed and the front door key in a special ceremony.

But if I ever hope to get rich, I've got to buckle down to my studies. Sometimes my mind wanders off and I lose track of what I'm reading. Last Monday I complained at breakfast, "I have to read some dumb old poem, real long, for English."

"What was the reading matter assigned you?" Granny Grand wanted to know.

"Oh, this old thing called *The Lady of the Lake.*"

"Sir Walter Scott's *Lady of the Lake*?"

She leaned over and looked hard into my eyes. Gazing back into hers, those dark pupils with the pale blue rings, I got the feeling that for just one second she had lost all hope for me.

That night after supper she brought out one of the little volumes she's covered in MacLean plaid and said: "Now, I'd like to read you my favorite portion of *The Lady of the Lake*."

She explained that she was reading the scene where Ellen Douglas goes to the king to seek her father's release from prison. Fitz-James, knight of Snowdoun, goes in with her. I remember Fitz-James was that guy who popped in and out of Ellen's life and was trying to help her get her father back. Something about a ring.... So here was this Fitz-James, "Snowdoun's graceful knight," leading Ellen into the king's court, "a thronging scene of figures bright." Granny Grand read, her voice trembling a little:

> On many a splendid garb she gazed
> Then turned bewildered and amazed,
> For all stood bare, and in the room
> Fitz-James alone wore cap and
> plume.

She paused, watching me closely. Did I understand? she seemed to ask.

"Miss Evans hasn't explained that part to us yet," I told her.

She went on:

To him each lady's look was lent,
On him each courtier's eye was bent;
Midst furs and silks and jewels sheen,
He stood, in simple Lincoln green
The centre of the glittering ring —
And Snowdoun's Knight is Scotland's
King!

And when she read out in a trembly voice that last line, I felt an electric current run from my neck all the way down to my tail bone.

"Could you read that again?" I asked.

And she did.

I never thought I'd memorize poetry Miss Evans hadn't assigned, but I've learned thirty lines of what I used to call "this dumb old poem," and sometimes when I'm just walking along, I say to myself, "And

Snowdoun's knight is Scotland's king" and get that same thrill down my backbone.

Chapter 10

1938

THE CRY OF THE OWL

Flora and I are talking about the owl again. Or what *I* think was the owl but what she still thinks of as some big mystery. She tells me for the hundredth time, "You used to point to the woods and say, 'olie tonight, Flora, olie tonight.' And I'd ask your mama, "What *is* that child trying to tell us?"but she didn't know, no more than I did. You'd almost cry when we couldn't understand what you were talking about."

"It was the owl, Flora. I'm sure it was the owl I was talking about."

There's a screech owl in our woods, and it has the most awful cry. Unearthly, Granny says. To me it sounds like a woman being strangled. Croaking as the rope is drawn tight, screaming as the strangler lets up.

"It must of waked me in the night when I was little and scared me half to death."

Flora keeps right on fixing dinner — stuffed bell peppers and some kind of potatoes and fresh green peas and beefsteak tomatoes grown against the brick wall. I'm chopping the onions and celery for the stuffed peppers. Flora makes me clamp a wooden match in my teeth when I chop onions so I won't cry so much.

It's funny about me and Flora. When I was little, I thought she was like an aunt, a member of my own family. I never even noticed her color. But the first time she brought Charlie Mae to our house, I wet my finger and rubbed it on her knee to see if the color would come off. "Blue knees," I said, and all the grown-ups laughed.

"Colored people," most white people

call them. Granny Grand sometimes calls them "darkies." The first time I used the word *Negro*, Granny said, "The way you say it, it's too close to *nigger*." (You can get your mouth washed out with Octagon soap for saying *nigger* in this house.) *Knee-grow* is how Granny pronounced it and made me say it after her several times.

When I was still little I began to notice that Charlie Mae never went to the Pickwick with me but to her own theater in a wooden building that used to be a colored church. *Why?* I kept asking Flora about things like this. And *Why not?* Like when she'd take me to Threadgill's Pharmacy and say, "My little lady here wants an ice cream soda," then stand behind my chair. "You sit down with me, Flora," I'd say, and the men behind the counter would laugh. Then they'd give her a cup of ice cream to take home. All Flora could say to my *why*'s and *why not*'s was: "Because that's the way things *are*."

Now, of course, I understand how we're still coming out of slave times and things move slow. Even Granny Grand says slavery was a great wrong. "And they *still* live in cabins," I told her once. And she could only shake her head.

Flora puts out the parboiled peppers and grated meat. I help her shell the peas.

"I don't guess you remember that time you locked yourself in your papa's study," she says.

"Oh but I do, Flora, I remember it perfectly."

Well, maybe I don't remember it *all*, but I've heard the story so many times and made up little things to go with it that it's become every bit as good as memory. And I remember clearly how it changed the way I looked at Flora.

I must have been about four years old and was wearing my hat with the ro-ses, even though there was snow on the ground. It was back when Granny still ran the Spinning Wheel Shop and Mama was at her office and Granny Grand had not come to live with us yet. Flora must have been real busy that day and just let me wander.

I went upstairs and into my daddy's study. That was before Mama had to make it into a bedroom so we could rent out her room. Back then it had bookcases along all four walls and Daddy's portrait above the coal-burning fireplace. He had on the uniform he wore in the Great War, and he was not smiling. His blue eyes followed me wherever I went in that room. Even behind his file cabinet — I'd peek out, he'd still be staring. Granny told me that I used to talk to the portrait and bring things to show it. Maybe that's why Mama took it down and hung first a sampler, then two years ago King Edward's Farewell, where it had been.

Anyway. I closed the study door and for some reason locked it. Or maybe I'd turned the key before, only this time the lock clicked into place. It didn't scare me that I was locked in. In fact I kind of liked it. I went over and picked up a few pieces of coal from the bucket and laid them on the rug. Then I went to look at the snow in the yard and on the porch roof, which was right outside one study window. That snow was pretty deep. I examined my daddy's pipes, still lined up on his roll-top desk, and in his magnifying mirror I studied every rose on my hat.

And then I heard Flora calling. She called all the way up the stairs, and I could hear her opening every door to every room and closet. When she got to the study door and found it locked, she said, "Miss Mariah, open up this door."

Instead I took out the key and looked through the keyhole at her eye, staring into mine. We looked at each other for about a minute this way, and then I heard her go back downstairs. She came back up and started making a lot of noise in Granny's room next door. Then I heard a tramping. I went over to the window and saw her coming across the porch roof. The snow came up to the middle buckle of her galoshes. She walked over to the window and just stood there. And from here on I know I have an absolutely true memory. Seeing her like that, I suddenly realized how good she was, how *noble* (even though I didn't know that word yet, I still remember my exact feeling to this day), how noble she was and how bad I'd been to lock her out. I can still see her standing there in her old galoshes with her coat thrown over her shoulders, and that white cap she always wore, and her work apron, just standing there looking in at me.

I climbed on top of my daddy's wardrobe trunk and unlatched the window. She lifted it and stepped in carefully, first onto the trunk, then the floor. She stood looking at me through her fogged-up spectacles, then wiped them on her apron and looked at me some more. Finally she said, "You have caused me one heap of trouble *this* day, Miss Mariah."

And I said (and here the true memory continues), "I'm as sorry as I can be, Miss Flora." It was the first time I ever called her *Miss* and maybe the last time too. She sat down on the wardrobe trunk and bent over double. I didn't know whether she was laughing or crying. It sounded more like laughing, but she was wiping her eyes. Maybe she was laughing at my hat, still on my head, roses and all.

"Well," she said finally, "I got to get back to my work. So please give me that key."

I took it out of my pocket, and after she unlocked the door she put the key on top of a book case. I knew how to climb up to get it. But I didn't want to.

Flora is saying now, "Well, I guess I better get the lemon spongette started."

Whenever she promises me spong-ette — lemon or vanilla, it doesn't matter which — she can get lots of work out of me. Which is why I'm sitting at the kitchen table now, talking about the owl and other things of long ago and helping her with the dinner.

"It was the owl," I tell her once more. " 'Olie tonight' meant the owl, Flora."

She's not happy about the owl. She'd rather think that 'olie tonight' was some child secret I once had but forgot when I got big. Some deep knowledge children have that grown-ups can never understand.

Chapter 11

1939

THE MEN THEY LOVED
AND
THE MEN THEY MARRIED

Whenever I think about the women-folk in my family, that line that reaches down to me, I always start with Big Mother, Granny Grand's mother. "She could be a formidable lady," says Granny, whom she'd practically raised. Big Mother had only one arm; she lost the other at eighteen.

The way it happened was, she fell out of a swing and broke it. The local doctor didn't know how to set it right, and the arm finally had to be amputated. The surgeon fell in love with her —he was a good bit older — and she with him. They became engaged, but before the marriage could take place, he died.

The one photograph we have of Big Mother has almost the same face Granny has now, though sterner and sadder. She's dressed in a dark cape, which she wore to hide the missing arm. Granny Grand says she would pin her sewing to her skirt to keep it in place while she made tiny feather stitches. She didn't marry until her late twenties, which was practically an old maid in those days. Her husband was a gentleman with white mutton-chop whiskers and an upturn to his mouth that makes you wonder whether he was trying to smile or trying *not* to smile. There's an oil portrait of him but not one of Big Mother.

They had only two children — Granny Grand and her older sister Marianna, who was so brilliant that she took "the boys' course" at the academy they went to.

As for Granny Grand, she married the only man she ever loved, as far as I know. He was twenty years older than she was, just like my daddy was twenty years older than Mama. All three women in my house were married at nineteen, an age I'll be in four more years, though I can't believe *I'd* ever marry that young. Anyway, my great-grandfather was Scottish and came over as a boy to Nova Scotia, then on down to North Carolina, where he settled. I see him clear in my mind's eye standing on the deck of that Scotch ship, peering out to sea, looking for the new land and the new life he was moving towards.

By the time he met Granny Grand, he was a widower with a son one year older than she was, and I can see the three of them sitting around the supper table trying to talk to each other. How would you talk to a stepson your own age, or how would you talk to a beautiful stepmother whose eyes were as black as seven devils? All I know about this stepson is that he died in his mid-twenties and was referred to as "poor Malcolm."

Granny Grand adored Colonel MacLean, which is the name I give my great-grandfather whenever he comes into my mind. I have some trouble seeing him as all that noble, mainly because of the way he broke up Granny's romances. The first time was when she was a student at Mary Baldwin College. She had a friend named Hannah Epstein, whose brother Abram would stop for a visit whenever he was in the area. One time Hannah introduced Granny to her brother, and when he found out she was a music major, he asked her to play a Beethoven piece for him. She did, and he asked if she would play for him when he came again. She said she would.

Then one day Miss Baldwin, as formidable as Big Mother, called her into her office. Miss Baldwin was in the habit of saying, "Girls, I am shocked and mortified at your reprehensible behavior," which the girls in secret would drawl out to: "Girls, I am shocked, horrified, stultified, petrified, ossified..." and on and on ... "at your reprehensible, abominable, intolerable," ... etc., etc.... "behavior." So when Granny was summoned into her office, she assumed that it was for some reprehensible behavior like making snow cream in the dormitory, with theft of vanilla and sugar from the kitchen. Instead Miss Baldwin told her that she'd "been petitioned by, and given permission to, Abram Epstein to call upon you, provided this is agreeable to you."

And from then on scarcely a week passed that Granny did not see Abram Epstein. Of course Hannah and other girls were often with them, but he paid special attention to "Brownie," as everyone called

Granny, her full name being Mary Browning MacLean, waiting for a husband's last name to be added to it. Anyway. The feeling between them grew steadily, and when she went home for Christmas he gave her a gold locket and a picture of himself in a silver frame.

Poor innocent Brownie, she'd hardly arrived home before she opened her valise to show her mama and papa her gifts. Her papa strode over and took the picture out of its frame, and as though he was presenting evidence to a jury, said, "Now, Mary Browning, I want you to observe carefully what I am about to do with this picture." And he moved away the fire screen, laid the picture on the coals, and made her stand there and watch Abram Epstein's face burn up.

I don't know how she ever forgave him, or how Granny Grand could stand there and watch the whole thing. Furthermore, he wrote Miss Baldwin a sharp note forbidding his daughter to see the young man ever again. Whatever became of the locket, I don't know, but I like to think that it is in one of Granny's boxes, with a smaller picture of Abram Epstein still in it, and that some day I can open it and look upon his face.

Mama, when she told me this story, said it wasn't just because Abram Epstein was Jewish that my great-grandfather broke up the romance. He also got rid of the beau who presented the handkerchiefs with "Happy New Year" on them, and also the young man who every Sunday of one whole summer brought a watermelon with his initials carved into the rind. The Colonel could not abide the beau who drove his own buggy or the one who stayed until the Asheville train whistled past the east meadow, then bolted for the depot. He particularly disliked Ephriam Early, whom Granny called the Prince Charming of her life. The Colonel broke up that romance by appearing in the parlor every ten minutes with his gold watch in his hand.

And then as her nineteenth birthday came closer, the Colonel invited the new doctor over for Sunday dinner. "Mary Browning, I have found you a man worth marrying," he said.

And she did! I guess because she adored her papa and didn't hold it against him that he'd messed up her life. Maybe in those days that's just what fathers did. But I know *my* daddy would never have. Anyway. It was a pretty good marriage, as far as I can tell. Oh, I don't think she was fascinated with him the way she'd been with Abram Epstein, or loved him like she did Ephriam Early, but she appreciated him for being the good man he was and the father of her children. She told me the other day, "One should never marry the Prince Charming in one's life." I've been trying to figure out why not, but there's no use asking. This is part of her "inscrutable wisdom," as she always says about God.

Mama, just like Granny Grand, fell in love with a man twenty years older than she was — her English professor at Trinity College. She told me once: "He had the purest blue gaze I ever saw, and he would fix it on you when he asked questions like, 'What is Hamlet really saying to Ophelia in this passage?' He'd get me so rattled with those blue eyes of his that I'd have to struggle hard to keep my mind on the question and answer it properly."

He loved to work with tools. On Saturdays he'd put on his striped overalls and mend worn-out things or make new ones. One time he scared Mama half to death by climbing on the roof to replace some shingles. She was expecting me then and because of her condition became hysterical. He had to promise her he would never go up on the roof again as long as he lived.

Which wasn't long, sad to tell. He caught the flu that winter, went back to his classes too soon and came down sick again. Going into the pantry to make him a mustard plaster, Mama slipped on the waxed linoleum and fell, bringing on labor. I think of my daddy at home with only a nurse while we were in the hospital twelve miles away. He'd send over messages. "Where's the boy you promised?" was one. But he was only kidding. They did, though, think it would be a boy and were going to name him Patrick. I sometimes dream about that Patrick's life, with a live daddy and a brother or sister or two. But I've got my own household. A mother and a grandmother and a great-grandmother, and sometimes an uncle who comes to stay wherever we can tuck him in. Who says you have to have a family like everybody else's?

Anyway. My daddy caught pneumonia, and the night after my birth it went into double pneumonia and finally heart failure. The doctor told Mama that he'd asked, "Can this be it?" Surprised, because he'd expected to welcome us home, then get back to his books and do all the things he and Mama had planned out for our lives. I feel sorriest for her, but I feel sorry for him too, having to leave like that, not ready to go. And sorry for myself that I never got to meet him.

Come to think of it, I never knew a one of the men who are my ancestors. Portraits and books with notes scrawled in them and pongee hankerchiefs with their initials worked in the corners by the women who loved them, and their accounts of battles they'd been in and plaques commending their bravery and their learning — these are what I have of them. And their stories — yes, I have their stories too, told by the women who loved them.

Chapter 12

1940

THE HOUSE MY FATHER BUILT

Mama used to tell me, "This is the house your father built for you." I could see him in his striped overalls hammering a-way on the bookcases, lining up the bricks for the fireplaces, whittling the newel post that made its witch-head shadow every time I went upstairs to bed. What she meant was that he had worked with the architect to have every detail just right.

But by some "quirk of the law," as Granny put it, this house does belong to me. It was because my father didn't leave a will, and the law "protects the minor child." So when I come of age, I can turn everybody out and live all by myself in solitary splendor. Not that I would ever do such a mean thing. I don't know why that thought even popped into my head.

Mama has a big account book to put down all the money she spends on the house and on me. Then every so often she has to show it to some dumb old judge who's keeping track of every nickel she spends. The first page reads:

Record of dwelling at 637
E. Jefferson Street, owned
by Mariah Thorne, minor, to be
administered by Mildred G.
Thorne, Guardian.

And then there is a recent entry:

Sum of $3,000, represent-
ing first mortgage on dwelling
at 637 E. Jefferson Street, for
the education and maintenance
of Mariah Thorne and for necessary repairs and improvements
to preserve her property.

Then there are checks for new
grates for furnace and installation,
$20.70; and repairs on shower bath and
new shower head, $3.12. Stuff like that.
The rest of the mortgage money is put away
for my college education, though every now
and then I see a check recorded for things
like: to Smith and Edmonds, Jeweler, for
mounting ring for Mariah out of diamond
stickpin belonging to her father and for re-
stringing her pearls, $18. And to Franjeans,
dress, sox, bag, flower, $10.

She keeps the account book in the
secretary and tells me any time I want to
look at it I can. I'd rather not know about all

this, to tell the truth. How the law gave me what should have been *her* house and then makes her record how much every nail or plank costs and every haircut, every pair of anklets, for me. If I had to do that for a child of mine, I'd be awful cross and snappy. But my Mama doesn't complain. And she treats me out of her own pocketbook every time we go out. One time when I'd ordered an awful lot at the Coffee Shop, I told her, "Why don't we just take this out of my inheritance?" and she got that look like when she's trying to keep from laughing. She paid the bill herself, counting out all her pennies.

In a way the house has never been all ours, "to enjoy in privacy," as Granny says. Since I was three years old Mama rented out the suite — two rooms and a bath — that she and my daddy planned to use themselves. And I have the little room that was to have been her sewing room. She's taken over my daddy's study — sold the roll-top desk and bookshelves and moved in a chifforobe and beds. Sometimes we rent out that room and mine too to the dancing girls who come for the University dances. So the house is not what my daddy planned at all. When I was little I used to wonder where we'd put him if he ever came back. I was really dumb in those days and figured maybe he could use the Texas bed in the attic, where Uncle Eric sometimes sleeps, and where Mama and I stay when the dancing girls come. "I hope you won't have to live like this when you grow up," she told me, last time we slept in the Texas bed. But I don't mind, especially when there's rain and we listen to the sound of it on the roof right over our heads.

And I just plain love it when the dancing girls come. Their sweet smells and high voices fill the house. Their "ball gowns," as Granny Grand calls them, hang from ceiling fixtures, and they comb out their long and shining hair. Then the college boys in their tuxedos come down the hill with corsage boxes under their arms, and they and the dancing girls walk back up the hill arm in arm or holding hands, their laughter floating behind them.

The thing that really upset me was when we had to rent out the whole house and move to a lot of little places. But Mama was able to get a hundred and fifty dollars a month for our house and pay out only thirty dollars for the little places. We rented the house first to the Adamses, a young couple whose families had heaps of money. Once on the streets of New York City, when Alex and Susan Adams were strolling just a few days before their wedding, a man ran up and shot Alex in the stomach, and their wedding had to be postponed. I thought about that shooting every time I saw him and marveled that he'd lived.

Then we rented to the Forresters, people older than Mama but not quite as old as Granny. He wrote books about lost civilizations and she wrote cookbooks, so I guess they had some money but not as much as the Adamses had, for they couldn't pay but a hundred dollars a month. That was the time we moved to one of Jack Edney's country cottages, which we got for only twenty dollars. I was dying to ride the school bus when we lived out there, and finally Mama let me, but Bud Crabtree threw up all over my new shoes, so I never asked to ride it again.

Anyway. When we moved back to Jefferson Street after the Forresters left, the place was jumping with fleas from their two collie dogs. We had to go up to the mountains to visit relatives while the exterminator gassed the house. Mama wrote the Forresters and asked them to pay the bill, but Mrs. Forrester wrote back that the fleas must have been due to "spontaneous generation."

"That settles it," Mama said, "I will

never rent out this house again." And I was so happy I danced through all the rooms rejoicing.

Of course we still had to rent out the suite, and the grannies moved down to the dining-room so their room could be rented too. From then on we ate only in the breakfast room.

But there's the porch, good as an extra room. It's like a tree house, right in the woods. And there's this swing my daddy designed that looks like a spool bed with its legs sawed off and the headboard made into the swing's back. After supper, except in winter, Mama and I go out and sit there and listen to the wood thrushes sing their *tootle-loo*s and *tootle-lay*s. When I was little, I'd always go to sleep with my head in her lap, and she'd carry me up to bed. But now I sit in the matching rocking chair while Mama takes the swing. Sometimes there is a sadness to this porch, this house. I feel it now.

Mama has not been herself lately. "Her mind is overrun," Flora said when Mama put last year's date on her check.

"Lately," Mama says now, "I think about your father a lot."

Maybe about how he never got to sit on this porch, in this swing, creak back and forth, listen to the wood thrush chorus. How he never got to hold his baby in his arms. If she ever started weeping for the gone men in her life, she'd weep a whole year. Her beloved papa. Her strong brother, my Uncle Tandy. Her husband, my daddy. A neighbor, a widower, the one man she might have married, killed in a fire. All of them gone.

"I know," I say to her. Best I can do.

She lights another Camel. We sit listening to the wood thrushes till dark.

Chapter 13

1941

CHARLIE MOCK
AND
OTHER MIRACLES
OF THE SEVENTEENTH YEAR

Last week I "turned seventeen," as Granny Grand says. As though I'd turned a corner or walked into another room. And in a way I have. The braces are off my teeth. I don't have to smile my u-shaped smile anymore. Now I can have a smile like June Allyson. But when your top lip's not been lifted for three solid years, it gets sort of paralyzed. "I'll Never Smile Again" is not my favorite song right now.

Actually Mary Lou's more the June Allyson type than I am. I'm dark and mysterious like Merle Oberon, and my smiles will be rare but dazzling. I practice smiling slowly, wider and wider, higher and higher, while saying, "Yes, that's *right*," pretending some fraternity man has just said my name. Provided I ever meet a fraternity man. Provided he would want to know my name.

It's not exactly what I'd hoped for but it will have to do. Buddy Lisle has invited me to a University dance. The May Frolic. He's only a freshman — last year he was a senior in high school just like I am now. I've known him all my life. His grandmother and Granny Grand knew each other in the Naomi and Ruth Circle of the Wilton Presbyterian Church centuries ago. Well, decades. And there are other connections I haven't the strength to go into. He's considered something of a drip but he *is* an ATO. Mary Lou says they rushed him because an ancestor of his helped found the fraternity. A *legacy* is what Buddy is. The reason I said yes when he asked me is that he is my ticket to get into the world of college boys — or rather, university men. And besides, Tommy Dorsey's playing.

I found some flowered chintz — moss roses and carnations on an ivory background with lots of ferns thrown in — and Mama assisted by the grannies is making me a "ball gown," as Granny Grand calls it.

Here is their conversation:

"It's a good thing she's so thin or she'd look like an overstuffed chair in this chintz." (Mama)

"Oh Midge..." (Granny, always taking up for me.)

"What dances do the young folks do these days?" (Granny Grand, changing the subject)

"I suppose the Big Apple's gone out by now." (Granny)

"It was rather like the Virginia reel, didn't you think?" (Granny Grand)

"Amazingly similar." (Granny)

"Oh, they've run through the Big Apple and the Little Apple too and are now jitterbugging." (Mama)

"I *see*." (Granny Grand means to make a study of jitterbugging, I can tell.) "Midge, did you ever dance the Charleston?"

"Oh yes, back in the dark ages." And Mama calls me in for a fitting.

The Tin Can, which I've only been to for basketball games, tonight is dark and mysterious. Too many balloons, Buddy

Lisle complains. I'm afraid he's going to be more of a drip than I realized. I'm wearing flat heels so I won't be too much taller, but still I have to bend down whenever he says something.

Chintz is definitely *in* this year, but mine's the prettiest of anyone's. Perfect with this moonstone necklace and fake gardenias that glow in the dark. And shoes dyed to match the ferns in the dress. I see guys giving me interested looks. Most of the ones who look my way I ignore. But there's this one boy — man, really — whom I'd give anything just to have glance in my direction. His name is Charlie Mock — "Cholly," his fraternity brothers call him. A Deke and head cheerleader — that's Charlie. At football games I watch him, dressed to kill in his white flannels and monogrammed sweater with this giant megaphone he uses to get the crowd to roar like one giant beast. The throb of the band makes an answering throb in my chest, but I feel another kind of throb every time I look at Charlie.

I've watched Charlie leaning against the door frame of the Sartor Resartus Men's Shop, where he works part time, and once I got up the nerve to go in and price belts, but it was Charlie's day off. And whenever Mary Lou and I put on our act in front of Threadgill's Drug Store to attract the college boys, I always glance down the street to see if Charlie is standing outside the Sartor Resartus listening.

"Mariah Thorne," Mary Lou will shriek, "do you mean to tell me you live at the far end of East Jefferson Street and you've never visited the Troll's Fountain? — why, it's almost in your back yard!" (Name and — practically — address.) Or she'll shout out as we pretend to say good-bye: "Your phone number's still 6331, isn't it?" When you consider it was 6331 three years before either of us was born, this would seem like a pretty dumb question to

138

any listening townsperson. But Mary Lou and I aim only at the college boys' ears. Then of course I return the favor and shout out *her* phone number for Charlie himself maybe to pick up and call her instead of me. Which would just kill me, it really would.

Anyway. Here is Charlie at the May Frolic. I watch him circulate. He seems to have come alone — no date — and he's looking the girls over. But just before he gets to me, the band begins to play "Fools Rush In."

"Well, guess we oughta dance," says Buddy, like it was some harvesting chore we had to do.

He does a one-two-three-four, over and over, making those boxes, like we learned to do in Mrs. Von Eberle's House of Dance, though most of us went on to more ambitious steps. I notice a line of boys standing behind us — watching, smiling. Then the first one in line steps up and says

"Hey, Buddy, won't you introduce us to your pretty little girl there?"

I'm not so little, I want to say but smile instead. It's coming back, my smile; I feel it. I'm getting the hang of how to do it. "A smile in full radiance" — those words come to me. But almost before the first boy and I can get started, the second one taps his shoulder and says, "May I cut in?" and then the third and on and on. What is this anyway? Some sort of joke Buddy's fraternity brothers are playing on him? Is this a late initiation? The line gets longer and longer and I see one boy I've seen lounging around in front of the Deke house. So they're not all ATO's. Then I realize, this is the stag line! The stag line giving *me* a rush.

And now the band starts playing "Green Eyes." A really good dancer breaks in on me, and off we go whirling around the dance floor, me smiling with my new and perfect teeth. Then there is a marvellous voice saying, "Time's up, friend!" and Charlie Mock is breaking in on me! I think I may faint, but I must play it cool; let him think I've had all the Charlie Mocks of the Western World dancing with me. He leans over and smells the gardenias in my hair. They glow beautifully in the dark but smell of sulphur. Charlie smiles like an elf and looks at me sideways. "I'll never tell your secret, ma'am," he says. And we start to dance. But suddenly I trip, and Charlie has to steady me. Will he think I did this deliberately, just to get him to hold me tighter?

"Oh, I see what the trouble is," he says, "your hem's come out. Let me sit you down and fix it with some tape..."

Must be the part of the hem I sewed — my stitches too loose, Granny always says.

Charlie leads me to a folding chair, then rummages in his pockets. Instead of a tux he's wearing a midnight blue jacket with built-in belt and pockets that must run from hip to knee. Out of these amazing pockets he begins to take things and lay them in my lap: a pocket knife, a wad of string, a book of postage stamps, a penny post card.

"Aha!" And he holds up a roll of adhesive tape, then takes the knife which miraculously has a tiny pair of scissors built in, cuts a strip and fixes my dress.

"That'll hold for awhile," he says.

I hand him back his things and watch him drop them in his pockets. There is something about these things of his and his deep pockets and the way he knelt to fix my dress and his man's voice that makes me know I'll have to have him no matter what it takes.

"So shall we dance now?" Charlie asks.

"If we go back on the dance floor, the boys will just start breaking in," I say.

And Charlie begins to laugh. He slaps his thigh, makes a rattle in his pockets, and repeats my line about the boys breaking in. Finally his laughter sighs out and he says: "You're the only girl I ever met who doesn't want anyone to cut in."

"But Charlie," I say, "I'd much rather just sit here and talk to you."

And he stares at me for what seems like a full minute, his face gone serious and a little sad. I can't quite read his expression, but I think it's part pity, part wonder, and part love. I wait, hoping.

And then he says: "You're too pretty to be sitting here like a wallflower, so I'll just take you over to a corner where nobody will bother us, O.K.?"

We dance in the shadows, and every now and then I see boys prowling over, but Charlie must give them some signal because they drift away again.

"I guess you're stuck with me," I say.

And he leans back to study me. "No nicer gal to be stuck with," he says.

We only dance to the slow numbers: "The Breeze and I," "Blue Champagne,"

"Maria Elena." Charlie hums along; the notes drift into my fake gardenias. Which of all these numbers will become "our" song, Charlie's and mine? Or am I rushing things?

We sit out "Tangerine," but my feet dance sideways, like Granny Grand's do when she sits with the cat in her lap listening to Phil Spitalny and his All- Girl Orchestra. My feet dance faster and farther than hers, and Charlie, watching me through the smoke from his cigarette, declares he's never seen anyone dance sitting down before.

After we get up for "Embraceable You," Charlie says: "If you weren't such a young thing, I just might come courting you."

"I'm not all that young." And I give him a rare but dazzling smile.

"So then. What's your phone number?"

"6331." I say the numbers slow and clear so they will click into place in his brain.

"Got it," he says and leads me back onto the dance floor. But the stag line doesn't pester us any more.

Chapter 14

1941-42

THE FULLNESS OF LIVING
WITH DEATH CLOSE AT HAND

Here I stand in my dark room looking up the driveway, waiting for Charlie. He broke our first date because Buddy Lisle told him I lived with my mother, my grandmother, and my great-grandmother. Buddy wasn't being mean — just answering Charlie's questions. But Charlie must have panicked, because he called me with some flimsy excuse. Broke the date. Then last week he called to make another one. Still, I'm nervous he won't show up.

But here he is! Galloping down the hill, his jacket thrown over his shoulders like a cape. My life will never be the same after tonight. That thought comes to me, and I'm joyful and sad all at the same time. I put on a little more Shalimar, then go down slowly.

"Come right in," Granny is saying. "Mr. Mock, isn't it? We used to know a family of Mocks lived just over the Tennessee line." Charlie answers her like there's nothing he'd rather talk about at this moment than remote kinfolks who moved from western North Carolina into Tennessee. "Ben Mock." Granny seems to be drawing a picture in her mind. "I used to know him well. He courted one of my sisters." Granny can go on like this all evening. Charlie is saying his *yes ma'am*'s and *no ma'am*'s like a good hometown boy.

I go in. Charlie looks up and says,

like he's never seen me before, "Well hello there!" and comes over and takes my hand. I know we've got to exit fast, or Granny Grand will start asking him about the Morrisons, whom Charlie has just said were "a lateral branch of the family." Granny Grand is great on anyone with the last name of Morrison. Charlie and I will have to name our first son Morrison Mock.

"I won't keep her out late," Charlie promises, and we escape. "Lovely ladies," he tells me and seems to mean it.

We go to Music under the Stars, held in the football stadium. Records, not live musicians, but still it's nice. Charlie spreads his jacket for me to sit on. Music under the Stars, Mary Lou says, is just an excuse to neck. But Charlie doesn't pull any fast ones on me. Once I put my hand on his knee to call his attention to a Tommy Dorsey number we danced to at the May Frolic, and he studies my hand, then looks into my face with that same wise, half-sad expression he'd had when I told him I'd rather sit and talk to him than dance with other boys. As we walk to the Dairy Bar, he calls me "little girl."

He doesn't even try to kiss me when he brings me home. He just brushes my hair back over my shoulders and asks if I'm busy Saturday night. "I don't believe so," I say, trying not to sound too eager; and we make another date.

For six months Charlie and I go on like this, but with things getting a little hotter each time. And we go to lots of movies. Charlie brings a box of Kleenex for when I cry. *Dark Victory* I've seen seven times and cry every time. Then after the movie we go to Hoffsheimer's Old Vienna Coffee House and sit under the sign that reads "On Reviens Toujours a Son Premiere Amour." Charlie asks me to translate it for him, pretending he doesn't know French, and I tell him, "One always returns to one's first love." He commends me on my grammar: "A lot of people would say, always returns to *their* first love, and that's incorrect."

I love to get Charlie talking about his life. He's the oldest of four children, with three sisters. "My parents took pity on me and let me build a roost in the attic." He used all the discarded furniture that was already up there, including an iron bedstead and a smoking stand with a little door. He even built a skylight, which leaked a little during heavy rains, so he had to move his bed out from under it and have buckets handy. He tacked pictures to the slanting ceiling, but you can't see them unless you lie down on his bed or on the rug his grandmother hooked for him. I love his talk. He said, for instance, that a rich uncle had passed on a Brooks Brothers' overcoat to him, and his mother "whittled it down to my size."

When we talk about my family, Charlie puts on a puzzled frown. "Now let's see—there's your mother and your grandmother and your great-grandmother..." It's like he wants to be sure he's got them all — maybe there's a great- *great-* grandmother up in a room somewhere. Or a sister off in college. Maybe a brother...

He can never pronounce my name. He makes *Mariah* sound like a cat howl. So we've come up with a new name, *Mari*, and I like it so much I've asked all my friends to call me by it.

Charlie's big-man-on-campus but also town pixie. A lot of people are Charlie watchers. "Ole Cholly — guess what he's done now?" And out comes another Charlie Mock story. Some are true and some are tall tales. Lately the talk has been about "Cholly's girl," or so Buddy Lisle says. Far from resenting Charlie's moving in on him at the May Frolic, Buddy's proud to have presented someone who caught Charlie's eye.

Actually I just may be Charlie's *only*

girl, because before me there'd only been "Cholly's women," and these are now my enemies. Whenever I see a co-ed staring at me real hard, I know she got the word, *that's Cholly's girl.* His choice of a high school senior (and one of the tall tales has it that I'm a high school sophomore who recently went to New York to audition for the Pied Pipers — me who can't rub two notes together without getting one wrong): anyway, his choice of a high school student may be an insult to University womanhood, but it's awful nice for me.

Sometimes Charlie and I double-date with Mary Lou and Cruise Hooper, the football player. He has a yellow Hudson convertible and sometimes even on winter nights he puts the top back and we all wrap up in blankets and go riding out the Reynolds Road, then beat the wind back home.

Cruise is not much of a talker. He has only about five things he says. One of them is "There you go!" and another, "Fine as wine."

When I ask Mary Lou if she's going to go steady with him, she says: "Heavens no, he's much too uncouth!"

But when he comes out on the football field, he looks graceful as a dancer and the crowd goes wild, like one huge animal roaring *Cru*-za, *Cru*-za, *Cru*-za! with Charlie leading the chant through his megaphone that's almost as big as him. And the old hound dog mascot wearing his blue and white saddle with sometimes a monkey riding on it is run round and round the field, and I notice Mary Lou yelling for Cruise as hard as anybody else.

And then sometimes Charlie borrows Cruise's car and takes me out to the old Pendergraft place, now no more than two charred chimneys standing on a triangle of land with three giant oaks. Someday, Charlie swears, he's going to buy this lot and build us a house with his own hands, and we'll live there until we're old, surrounded by grandchildren. Part of Charlie really wants this dream, but another part wants to get back to his women, who will neck all night with him and maybe even go all the way. But Charlie and I have to stop just when things get hot, and sometimes I have to ask him to take me home. But still, he comes back.

It's December already; today is the 7th. A Sunday like a dozen others, I'm thinking as Charlie and I come out of the Pickwick Theatre, leaving behind the smells of popcorn and dirty socks and the students' jeers and catcalls. We're shivering a little, and I've got that unreal feeling I always get when I come out of a movie into sunlight and my own ordinary world again. I expect it to at least be dark outside and maybe even full of London fog. As Charlie and I debate whether to go to the Dairy Bar or home to play some Glen Miller records, up rushes Buddy Lisle shouting, "Hey Cholly, did-ja hear — the Japs bombed Pearl Harbor!"

A dark look crosses Charlie's face, and he crushes out the cigarette he's just lit. "Damn," he says. "Damn it all." He takes my arm a little roughly, and we walk down Jefferson Street. At my gateway he stops, lifts a foot onto the rock wall and pinches off pieces of the browned bush that in spring will bloom again with lilacs. "Well, Mari, I guess we might as well get married."

It's not much of a proposal, but it's the best Charlie can do for now. "O.K., Charlie," I say. (Not the best acceptance either.) Somehow it doesn't seem the time for words. We kiss, and Charlie turns back toward campus.

Something keeps me from announcing my engagement at home. The grannies have just heard the news and are bent toward the radio, waiting for H. V. Kaltenborn to speak to them.

For awhile after Pearl Harbor Sunday Charlie disappears from my life. I look for him in all our old places, and when he's not in any of them, I get a preview of what it will feel like after he's gone to war. I'm not sure I'll be able to stand it. People shouldn't have to hurt this much. And then I think about Mama, after Daddy died, and I know now how she must have felt.

Words keep coming to me — "doomed by love and war alike." Did I read that in a book somewhere, or did I make it up? And since Josie Mason Bates read selections from "The White Cliffs" in chapel, these words keep coming back to me: "Lovers in peacetime ... (something, something) ... can question what to give. But lovers in wartime had better understand the fullness of living with death close at hand."

Finally Charlie calls to tell me he's enlisted in the Army Air Corps. "So when will you be called up?" I ask.

"Pretty soon," he says, "pretty soon."

He says that *pretty soon* like he's offering me reassuring news, news I'll be relieved to hear. But I go into my room and cry for an hour, and Granny has to call me twice to supper.

When I see Charlie again he repeats the proposal but wonders, because of "your extreme youth," whether we ought to get secretly married, then announce it later, after everything calms down a bit.

"And when will that be?" I ask.

"Maybe never. But we'll present them with a *fait accompli*."

I have no trouble translating — not the French, not the *them*, which I know means *Mama*. If we told her we were getting married, she would ask solemn questions and gaze at us with her dark eyes (black as seven devils, like Granny Grand's) and say my name in that drawn-out way of hers. Lately she's been assuring

158

me that there is money for my college education and that I must go away to a girls' school for at least two years before enrolling in the University.

Although the grannies have fallen in love with Charlie, Mama sees him as the enemy. A grown man come to take away her little girl. "If your father were here..." she said the other day, then didn't finish the sentence.

So yes, an elopement seems the only answer. Charlie is cheered that I agree, and the next time we see each other, he has the plan: he and Mary Lou and I will go down to Chesterfield, South Carolina, for the Christmas holidays with Cruise Hooper. Mary Lou and I will stay at his sister's house while Charlie stays with Cruise at his parents'. "Not even under the same roof"— Charlie gives me that line that I carry straight to Mama. And Cruise's sister sends a proper invitation. So Mama sighs and says a reluctant *yes*, then goes off to her room to smoke a Camel in the dark.

The grannies, though they'll "sorely miss" me at Christmas, are excited that I'm having such a glamorous trip and bring out my "Santa Claus," a muskrat coat and matching hat. I know what's gone into this purchase: part of Granny Grand's widows-of-Confederate-veterans pension, fifty boxes of Granny's candy and twenty-three of her fancy cakes, ten dissertations Mama typed after working hours, and donations from far-flung relatives. I wrap myself in fur, then sit down on the floor and cry.

Charlie is his old self again — planning, planning. "South Carolina is the easy-marriage state," he tells me, and adds that Cruise's brother-in-law, a lawyer, will help us get the license. He goes home to tell his parents, swearing them to secrecy, and brings back his grandmother's Tiffany ring, which she left in her will "for my grandson Charles' chosen bride."

"They loved your picture," Charlie

says, "and they love everything I told them about you, and they're all for us. If you should ever need a place to live while I'm in the Air Corps, you'd have a home there."

A knife slices through me. Leave Mama, leave the grannies, to go live with in-laws? But maybe that's what "cleaving only unto him" means — those words I heard just last week at Mary Lou's cousin's wedding.

The day we leave for South Carolina Flora packs us a picnic lunch. She fills a stationery box with pocketbook rolls, and when I see them, all warm and buttered, I burst into tears. She lets me cry, then puts a hand on my shoulder and says, "Now remember who you are and remember where you come from."

She's barely finished this speech when Cruise pulls his car up to the back door. Charlie leaps out and comes in for my bags, giving out his line of chatter to Flora, then to the grannies, who come to say good-

bye. They stand on the back porch, inno-
cently waving us off.

Mary Lou is wearing her new Christmas muskrat coat and matching hat just
like I am. Whenever we stand side by side
in our coats and hats, people tell us we look
like Rosemary and Priscilla Lane.

"Here..." Charlie pulls a small box
from his pocket and slips his grandmother's
ring on my finger. It had to go to the jeweler
for an extension. "They make fingers bigger than they did in Grandma's day," he
explains.

"Look..." I lean over and wave my
hand so Cruise and Mary Lou can admire
the ring.

"There you go!" says Cruise.

"Oh how beautiful!" says Mary Lou.

"Fine as wine!" says Cruise.

We drive past the north campus, the
Dairy Bar, the Old Vienna Coffee House,
the Pickwick Theatre. My life is spilling out
the rear-view mirror. *Stop!* I want to shout,

but Cruise keeps on, like he's moving toward some far-off goal post.

"Well, Mari," Charlie says. He takes my hand, like he knows what I'm feeling.

"Well, Charlie," I say back to him.

And we keep on travelling.

ABOUT THE BOOK

This book was composed and laid out on a Macintosh SE using Aldus PageMaker. It was set from disk at 1200 dpi in Postscript New Century Schoolbook by Southern California Printcorp of Pasadena, California. It was printed on 60-pound Thor Offset White acid-free recycled paper in Smythe-sewn signatures using soybean ink by Thomson-Shore Inc. of Dexter, Michigan. The four-color separation for the cover was made by Image Arts of Lansing, Michigan.

Any portion of the text may be reproduced with permission but without charge for use in Braille, large text, or audio versions for the handicapped. A copy of this and all other Signal Book titles are available free to Adult Literacy organizations through Student Coalition for Action in Literacy Education, UNC Chapel Hill, Chapel Hill, N.C. 27599.